Echoes of Poetry

Ishmail Penyai

CONTENTS

I SALUTE ZIMBABWE

It's full of honey
It's up to you
To harvest the honey
It's full of gold
It's the gold
It's full of diamond
Lets dynamite diamonds
To get to our destiny.

I salute Zimbabwe,
It's full of sons of the soil
till the land
Play with the soil
Money in the soil
Till the land
If you want to land
On real money
Liquid money.

I salute Zimbabwe
It's full of everything
With its full colours
It has coloured me
From top to bottom
It has coloured you
From birth to birthday
Happy 42nd birthday
My dear Zimbabwe.
Zimbabwe woyeeeeee!
My dearest Zim - Zimbabwe.

Colours of Zimbabwe
They have coloured me
Black and white
They have coloured me
With the rainbow colours.

The coloured
 and the non coloured
all colours matters most -
From Zambezi to Limpopo
From Cape to Cairo
It has coloured me
black and white
I like it black
Black is beautiful .

I like it red
Roses are red
Women like pink &red
I like it gold
It's not everything that's in gold
I like yellow
All my flowers
 flourish in yellow.
I like it in diamonds
My destiny is in diamonds.

I like it white
Peace to every family
Peace to all families
Peace to our communities
Peace to our country
Peace to our politics

Always portray –
  peaceful politics.

I salute Zimbabwe
I salute Zimbabweans
I salute - Zimbabweanism
Long live Zimbabwe
Long live Zimbabweans
Long live zimbabwenism
I salute you - Zimbabwe.

NEVER AGAIN

Never again
Same time
Next year
On next year.

Never again
On the dance floor
Two to tango
Not even one
Not even two
              to tango.

Farewell
To what could have been –
Tango dance
            of the decade.

I could have done –

with a dance.
You could have done
                        with a
                        contemporary dance
                                A caressing
dance
A Muchongoyo dinner dance

Go back to Chikore and Chirinda
Where all the dancers live
Without the wine.

Learn to read
Between the lines
 of life - everyday.

If you are not serving God

Who are you serving?
If you are not serving God
If you are not talking to God
Whom are you talking to?
If you don't believe in God
Who is your God

MARRY ME

I have asked you yesterday
To marry me-like yesterday
For you are
 everything to me.
Marry me
Before something else –
 marries me.

You were to me –
marriage material
Awesome material –
exciting material
Prayerful material
But now you are
             deceitful material
in my beautiful site.

My life begins with you
My day begins with you girl
I will marry you
For I have only seen you
A living marriage in making
And it's you –
Who makes me happy?
It's only you
Who makes me feel better?
My delayed days better
My delayed feelings better
My love life better.
But you are now unfaithful material
Now I am loading …
I am loading love

I am loading your love
My awesome days are here
Everything that is here
It all begins with you girl -
But you are no longer awesome.

The bond between attitude and altitude

Attitude and Altitude
Your attitude
Will determine your altitude
Fix your own attitude first
Your altitude will follow – flowing.

Fix your emotions –
Shungu neushungu zvakati siyane!
Fix your anger
 and bitterness
Fix your everyday mindset
Fix your punctuality
Fix your profound passion –
For other things.

A journey of a thousand miles
Begins with a time table.
Fix your time table
Fix your time
 and temper
Asante Sana -
 attitude and altitude

Asante Sana -
hustles of life
Hustle your life to infinite

FEARS FROM THE SPHERE

Fears in a tea cup
Fears-
 when crying
at a funeral.
Fears at a wedding
        Fears –
when you fall in love
        Fears
when you fall out of love
        Fears
 when disaster strikes
I dished out tears .
I cried
when I heard
about cyclone Idai.
I lost loved ones
In Chimanimani
In Chipinge
In Zimbabwe,
 Malawi and Mozambique.

There was profound fear
Throughout Southern Africa
During Cyclone Idai.

For every cup of tears you shed
God will replace them
With tears of joy.
May the lord replace our tears
With prosperous tears
 of eternal joy
From Ngangu
 right up to Khopa disaster
Cyclone Idai is a living disaster.

A person who understand your tears
Is much more valuable
Than a lot of people –
Who only know your smile.

As I travel through Machongwe
Nyabamba, Dzingire and Khopa
FEAR grips me profoundly
As I see these rivers flowing
Nyahode ,Nyabamba , Rusitu
All tears start flowing
and flooding again.

Blessing the hustler

Start hustling –
 not guzzling.
The lord blesses
 the hustler
and not the guzzler.

When you hunt
 you are hustling.
When you moan
you are mean.
But you don't moan
in the morning
Morning is for working
Work is for people
 who wake up
In the morning.

Moaning every morning
There is no solution
 In moaning every morning
May you please -
Stop moaning –
every morning.

Learn to hustle –
 in the morning
Hustle – every morning
Learn to live life
 to the fullest
Eyes on your passion –
 profoundly
Eyes on the prize

God is going to give you that prize.

Between passion and prize -
Perseverance and proceeds
Endurance and prosperity
Passion and patriotism
Peace and patriotism
Patience and humility -
Love and live
 your lovely life.

Asante Sana
 love and lovely life.

LOVE PROBLEMS

**Love problems –
Are life's problems.**

Look for problems
Solve the problems
There is money
In everyday problems.
The bigger the problem
the bigger the rewards.
Money is the reward
Go for problems
And get the money .
Move around

And identify problems
Move around
And make money - through problems.

GIRL YOU ARE

Girl you are –
 successfully saturated
With humour,humility and humanity
And a life to live today
So full of profound love
                    and laughter.

Wishes were horses yesterday
I wish I had met you yesterday
Morning without moaning.

Good morning my love life
Good morning my love life
There is no more moaning
Early in the morning.

When you see me moaning,
I am moaning with love.

Profound dreams

A beautiful woman
Bearing beautiful benefits
A beautiful woman I see
She just came from nowhere
And I was just somewhere
Waiting for her frivolous voice
coming from somewhere.

A beautiful woman –ooh –oh-oh
She was carrying all properties
Prayerful –
and romantic properties
Patience properties –
perspective properties
Prolific properties –
 potential properties
Patriotic properties.

I just like a phone call
She also had
            prepaid properties.

THE AUCTION IS OVER NOW

I am taken - today
The auctioneer was here- today
The auction is over - today
The race is over – today.

My shortest poem -
I have written it today
I have written it for you –
          today
The auction is over now.

Cherish this moment

Tears translate into love
Loneliness into living love
I fell in love
When I saw you - with love
I loved to love
And I live with love.
I chose to love

When I saw you - with love
I chose to love
And to live with love
When I saw you
 With living love.

I have chosen
 to love you
will you – love me?
If you love me
Please – don't leave me
Don't leave me – alone.

I WILL MARRY

When I want
Who I want
When she wants

I will marry –
the tallest woman.
She will bring me
A tall order - of happiness
The taller the better
 for the day.

I will marry
The shortest woman
Shortlisted for success
Shortlisted for efficiency
Shortlisted for brain work
Shortlisted for her charm
Shortlisted for her love
Shortlisted again –
 for her patience
 and presentation
Shortlisted for her perseverance .
Shortlisted for her passion
and patriotism
Passion and patriotism is key.

I will marry for

Patience,
        Passion
               and perseverance
I will marry for
Patriotism,
 Prayerfulness
 and prosperity

Those who pray –
 will prosper.
I will marry
 for prayer
I prayed
 and I got my prey.

Patriotism is a passion
Allow patriotism to prevail.
I love my country
I love Zimbabwe
I love my continent
I love my Africa.

I will marry
When I see symptoms
      of passion.
Passion for love
 and leadership
love have got its own leadership

Passion for patriotism
Passion for development
Passion for people and
egalitarianism

Love revolves around people
 and egalitarianism.
I will marry
Beyond egalitarianism

RIDDING ON RIDDLES

My first cycle
Was my riddle cycle.
I ride on riddles,
From my home village of Vhimba
Zvimba, Zhombeni and Zhombe.

I never fall on my cycle
It was an ancient cycle
Tried and tested for decades
Kureketa nemuti mukanwa
Upenzi hunonetse muna wahwo
Upenzi ngahunetse muridzi wahwo

Sandiwo ere mapenzi
 ari kunetseka nyamashi ngeupenzi?
Ungazopaema apo panoti mapenzi?

I like the riddle cycle
It's a cycle you ride with -
Humour, harmony and humility
It's a curious cycle
Full of imagery, satire and enemity
It fills you with profound laughter
And irons out the enemy of life

I love to laugh last
 with the least
The list of the last laugh is endless
I am still waiting to laugh
Not in vain .
I am still waiting
To love and laugh last
Prostitution has never thrived
 and survived
on profound procrastination.

Bye bye – to profound procrastination.

TRIALS, FEARS AND TRIBULATIONS

Trials will give you triumph
Fears will ferry you far
Fear of the unknown
I will make it known
And live without fear .

Cowards die a thousand times
Before their single celebration -
So said Shakespeare on writings

Patience will supersede
 And proceed to pay
For all your trials and fears.

When you hear the till ringing
It's time to pay Caesar.
When you see the notes
Paying in profound patience
and solace
It's time to pay me in silence.

A journey of a thousand smiles
It begins with a single smile
A journey full of prosperity
It begins with profound perseverance
Patience pays passion –
for its prosperity.

Follow your passion
And your money
will follow you.
I have said this several times
I will say it
 again and again.
Try try – try again
Try try – try again

Never say never
When it comes to trying
Try try – try again and again.

PURSUE PEACE AND OPTIMISM

The voice of the people
Is the voice of God.
Receive the voice
Sieve the voice
Recite the voice
Meditate on the voice

Laurels will never
Lift you up
Laurels will never
Lift you up without arms .
Don't go up in arms
Pursue the arm of God
Pursue patriotism
Pursue love and harmony
Pursue perseverance
And profound prosperity.

None but ourselves
Let's cease quarrels
Let's leave to quarrel
Action upon action
Zimbabwe needs action
Zimbabwe needs people
 with an action plan.
Optimism is the key
Patriotism is key
Egalitarianism must prevail
Prepare wonders to prevail

Patriotism is prosperity
Love what you do
Love Zimbabwe
 let's all love Zimbabwe
 today and tomorrow

I love Zimbabwe first
 our country Zimbabwe first.
My Zimbabwe first –
Others can queue
            until tomorrow.

CHALLENGES

Challenges will taste me
But will never eat me.
Challenges will taste me
But will never destroy me.
Challenges –
 real challenges
huge challenges
        have tasted me,
But failed to defeat me.

Challenges will taste you
But must never eat you .
Challenges will taste you
But never allow them
 to destroy you .

Challenges will go away
But please -
don't go away.
Challenges will show up
Like a dog chewing bones
But be bold
and be born again.

You will actually go far
Far-far away with challenges
Challenges will take you far away
Please don't stay too far away-
Challenges won't go far away.

COMMON SENSE

It takes passion
To have common sense
Passion for common sense.
It takes a good mindset
To adhere to common sense.
It takes six senses
To sense common sense ,
It takes two to tango .

Look around you everyday
See how far away people are
From common sense syndrome .
Their passion
to exercise and implement

The so called common sense.

Common sense is not cheap
And it will never be cheap
Common sense
 will never be common
Until people decide
 to use it uncommonly.

Acquire it
And acquaint to it
Asante Sana - common sense
Welcome to the club
Welcome to common sense
Thank you siyabonga-
 mwashuma
Twalumba

BEYOND YOUR KNOWLEDGE

Only God knows
There is one circumstance
That circumcised you.
There is harmony
That never harmonized you
There is one noise
that characterised You
 like now and again

Ask yourself why

do I make noise?
Why do people say
You are impolite ?
They repeat that
 now and again.
You must pity yourself
Put noise in a pit
 or armpit
Put impoliteness
    in a pit.
Put your agony
 in a deep pit.
Place your ego
 in ebony.

Only God knows
What secret you have
      Today
 and days behind.

Only God knows
What transpired to be
 what you are today?
A good boy
or a bad boy
A good girl -
carries greatness
A good girl
is moulded by God
I wish my daughter can be
A good girl
 throughout her life

I wish my two sons
a good behaviour
Good behaviour has
something to do with
 godliness and heavenliness.
May you please choose godliness
 and heavenliness.

God will find you
God himself created you.
When he wants to live with you
He will use you
 now and again .
When he sees you
                 being abused
He will love you –
beyond measure .
When you are living
 without love
He will smile with you.
When you live without leadership
He will shift and ship you
From Egypt to Canaan

Who doesn't want to go to Canaan?
Who doesn't want to live in Canaan?
The Canaanites were crying for Canaan
Moses was their middleman to Canaan

God will find you

When he wants to work with you
Through the journey to Canaan
Walk with God
If you want to walk
 through greatness.
Walk with God
If you want to walk –
 beyond greatness.

There was manna
On the way to Canaan
It was given to people -
with manners .
The manna had
its own manners
Even the angels
had their own manners
Do you have your own manners?
Not borrowed manners
I have never borrowed manners
I will never borrow manners
Except from God alone .

My pride belongs to God
Remain praying
and praying to God.

God himself will locate you
When he wants to write a book
He possesses the best handwriting
He will write what he wants
Through you .

He will say what he wants
Through you and all kinds of media
Whatsapp, Facebook,
  U tube – twitter - etc

You can name it
 day and night
God himself will rename it
And rename you.
God's time
is the best time .

Eyes on the prize
There is a prize
 on God's time.
There is always a prize
on God's prescribed time.

God will find you
Today or tomorrow or
       Yesterday.
He will pick you up -
From an unusual
 pick-up point.
He will walk with you
He will speak to you
From unusual places .
He will take you again
To unusual places everyday.

Always remember -
Whatever you do
Wherever you are

God will find you soon .

No matter what you say
No matter how hard
Your heart is hardened,
God will disconnect your hardness
Come rain even with thunder
God is busy - locating you
You will soon catch up
With his profound grace.

SOMETHING GOOD IS COMING

Famine will come
Don't stop –
  going to church
Challenges will come –
 day by day
Go to church everyday
Read the word everyday
Wisdom comes from the word

Pray until something happens
Pray until you see the sight of God
The same God who blessed you
Will bless me tomorrow
The same God who blessed you
Will bless you today and tomorrow
Only humility
 will take you beyond your ability.

Humility will never humiliate you –
May you please mark my words
Humility will never humiliate you
Humility will never late you down
Humility will never – pull you down

There is something coming - everyday
Keep preying on your prayers - everyday
Until something good comes your way
God is good and great everyday
Be thankful and grateful

When God blesses you -
Be humble
 and refrain from pride.
Be humble as usual
Be as humble as possible
And bless many more.
Many more will cry
for your blessings.
Bless them – as they come
Love them – as they come
Teach them again –
 as they come.

GOODBYE MY MENTOR

A family generation
A familiar generation
What is a family generation?
Where is a family generation?

A generation that generate love
And life with a purpose
The purpose of life
is to generate
A life full of love,
 laughter and prosperity
Who is here
to generate love and laughter?
Who is here for love and life?
Careless –they don't care
Care is decaying
 inside our hearts
Love is decaying
 inside your heart
Living a decayed love
 and life for decades

My second leg of life
It's full of love and life
My second leg of life
My final leg of life
It's full of harmony and humanity
My final leg of life
It's full of passion for patriotism
Passion for positive people
Passion for optimists.

My final leg of life
It's full of flowers and trees
Plant trees and flowers
 from your heart.
Plant some flowers
 full of love and life

Plant some flowers
 full of harmony and humanity
Don't forget to plant humility.

You left with everything
You are very selfish
You sell fish
And you are still selling fish.

You departed with everything
Everything that is called harmony
Everything that is called love
You took everything away from me
Selfish –you are very selfish
Wherever you are today
You just disguised
and went away
without a discussion
And left a trail
of lingering tears
Like a dog without an owner
Like a cat without a landlord
But the Lord remains
 my living shepherd.

Go away –
and own your love
Selfish love –
selfish –selling fish
Wherever you are
Selling fish –
 without a market.

The devil is a liar
A full time liar
And he will pay heavily
For whatever he did
 behind the scenes –
Mark my words
Hear my words
Nyamashi –
 ndareketa nemuti mukanwa
Musazoti andina mukanwa
Uyu ndiwo wangu mukana.

You went away with everything
Politeness, humanity,humility
 harmony and egalitarianism
 humanity and all your manners
I am left with nothing
I am left to mine nothing.

Humanity begins
 with a human being
Harmony and humility
Begins with you there
Peace begins
with you there
You will find peace
As you walk
on the global village.
I will walk –on the global village
In search of global peace
I will walk on this patriotic path
In search of refined patriotism.

You have to find peace
As you walk
 on the continental corridors
Patriotism begins with you there
Emit a percentage of patriotism
As you travel on the global village
Patriotism begins with you there
Patriotism begins with all of us here.
Instil peace and patriotism
In whatever you do
Wherever you go
Instil peace and patriotism
Whenever you can
Instil love and life
Whenever you can.
Instil peace of mind
If at all you mind.

There is no room for emotions
There is no living space
 for anger and the angry ones
There is no discovered market -
For bitterness, emotions and anger
Bitterness is not a business
Bitterness will always beat you
Always avoid – inflicted bitterness
Live life - with love and laughter

I have chosen to live life
With a profound difference
I have chosen to live with –passion
Peace, patience, perseverance
And profound prosperity

Live your life
 with a purpose for others
Live life with a successful legacy
A good name is a good legacy
Leave an immeasurable legacy.

My last leg of life
It's full of success
A journey of a generous generation
A journey that unfolds generosity
It begins with you.
A journey that generates generosity
A journey that unfolds generosity
It begins with you .
An egalitarian journey
The journey starts with you.

My mentor
 my memory verse
It all began with you.
A legacy of giving
When you give –
you are investing
When you give –
your cup overflows
With profound blessing
I resort to giving .

Charming brother
Your left me your charm
Honest and integrity –
you were very professional
Accessible like files –

accessible to anyone
Rewinding involves lots of things
Tears will run down my cheeks,
Life was good during your era.
You were good to everyone
Ever filled with humour
throughout your life
Sociable and responsible
 to all walks of life.

Goodbye – bye bye
My one memorable mentor,
Love you –
beyond measure.
I remember you –
 everyday
My mentor
My role model
Of my contemporary life.

GOD WILL FIND YOU

God himself will locate you
When he want to live with you.
He will use you -
When you are being abused.
People abuse people
How many have been abused
By close friends
And close relatives –

for their benefit?

He will love you -
 beyond measure.
When you are without love
He will smile with you
When you live
Without a successful smile.
You will smile
A non stoppable smile.
May God bless you
And me too -
With a non fiction smile.

God will find you
When he is in the laboratory
Doing what he knows best
Emotional distillation
Separating faith from fake
Separating truth from false
True religion from false one
God created this
 science and technology
So relax my brother and sister
Jesus is alpha and omega
Alfred and Ottilia can't match –
 his worthiness.
Adam and Oliver
can't beat his system
ndiye ega –
 Alpha and Omega

THE PASTOR'S PATH

The path
That the pastor use
It's called the pastor`s path
The path
That the pastor passes through
It's called –the pastor `s faith
The path
That the people pass through
It's called the people `s path
We all have a path
We all pass through a path
Different paths
With different people's path.

The pastor `s path
Where is the pastor
Where is the path
Who is the path?
The pastor `s faith
Who pays on the path?
Who likes the pastor?
Who walks with the pastor?

On his way to the pastor
The pastor `s faith
 will walk with the pastor
On this morning pasture

AN EAR THAT CAN HEAR

**Does your child have an ear
That can hear you?**
An eye that can see you?
A character
That characterises you?
Like father like son?
Like mother like daughter
Let there be dawn
On every daughter.
I declare dawn
On every global daughter.

An ear that can hear
May the lord grant us
That ear that can hear

An eye that can see
Far beyond our eyes
Far beyond our expectations.
An eye that can see
Far beyond
What you and I can see?
Far beyond
What all of us here
Can see and hear

May God grant us
 that opportunity
To hear

And see what is proper
An ear that can hear
The voice of God .
Hear and reciprocate
To the echoes of his calling
Do you hear
 the echoes of his calling?

From the mountains
God speaks through the mountain
He spoke yesterday and today
He is still speaking today
Like he spoke yesterday.

Wherever you are
There is an echo
Wherever you go
There is an echo in transit
I trust God
When the echo soliloquies
Alongside your silence.

Trust God
Alongside your new life.
There is a voice
Coming with a new voice
There is an eye
Coming with a new life
An ear with a new meaning
I want to hear whatever is new
Want to hear whatever is news
The news of Jesus Christ
The news without crisis

This is Jesus Christ
No more crisis
When you live in Christ.

SHE IS NOT AN EXCITING CHARACTER

She is not as exciting
As watching sun down
I would rather watch
                sun down.

She is not as lovely
As watching petunia flowers
In full blooming
I love flowers in full bloom.

She lives a dull life
With slow sense of humour
She carries along
An induced smile
But laughter is a way of life

She lives on borrowed laughter
I wish there was a market for laughter
A profound smile
And auction for action
And profound common sense

Life is a one off package
Love it well
Live without regret
Explore and exploit
I have explored
And I am exploiting everyday

FOLLOW HUMOUR

I always follow humour
Even when it is very humid .
Whether it is cold or hot
Laughter is the best medicine
A prescription without any cost

This is my story
A humorous story
This is my destiny
So full of humour
This is my success story
My story full of humour

HOT SPRINGS OF CHIMANIMANI

One of the wonders of Chimanimani
One of the wonders of Manicaland
One of the wonders of Zimbabwe ,

Hot Springs of Chimanimani
Ndauwe ndauwe –
 greetings from Chimanimani

I was there yesterday - in Chimanimani
Planting wonderful flowers and trees
I was there last Saturday
Seeing all sights of beauty

A stream flowing
With natural hot water
A swimming pool
full of hot water
Tape water flowing
With natural hot water
Can you believe this?

I do believe
Come to hot springs
In the heart of Chimanimani
Hot Springs of Chimanimani
One of the wonders of Zimbabwe

Hot springs of Chimanimani
God gave us this wonder
Wonderful hot water
Flowing in the kitchen tapes
Amazing waters of Chimanimani
A bath of natural hot water
God gave us this hot water
You can boil your eggs
Without switching electricity
Oh its time to save electricity.

You can have a cup of coffee
Without any heaters of electricity

Simply adding sugar
To hot springs water
You can have
A cup of tea
Simply add milk and sugar
To the waters of hot springs
Hot Springs of Chimanimani.
Welcome to tourism at its best
Welcome to Zimbabwe
A land flowing with milk and honey
Every day is full of milk and honey
You can have your honey
Whilst on your honey moon

Springs of hot water
Springs of natural hot water
Springs of Chimanimani
Springs of clean hot water
In the heart of Chimanimani
      hot springs
Springs of beauty
Springs in motion
Hot springs in motion
I am singing a song
For the hot springs in motion
Come to Chimanimani – in motion

A home
 away from home
There is a home

In the heart of hot springs
Chimanimani Hot Springs,
Lovely lodges
To launch a holiday
Lovely lodges
and a conference centre
For your convenient conference.
Fun fisheries
and mountain walk
Unleash a harmonized holiday
With an excursion to hot springs

Hot springs will give you
The air that you want to breath
The lease of holiday
That you want to have .
The harmony
That you would like to harness.
The beauty
That you want to carry
Back to your port of entry.
The holiday
That you want to hail
And herald
When you get back home.

The Bridal veil Falls in Chimanimani
You will fall in love
Before you fall
At the Bridal veil Falls
You will feel nature
Bridal veil Falls nature
Its first class nature .

Natural steep flow
I wish I can
 fly and flow
I have been here
At this falls
Love will never fall
When you are at the falls
It will uplift you at the falls.
Natural love falls
Allow it to fall and flow

Bridal veil Falls
Will give you the flow
That will lead you
To the falls
For a cup of living falls
That makes you flow.

Come to Bridal veil Falls
In the heart of Chimanimani
Come to Bridal veil Falls
The heart of Zimbabwe,s heart beat
With the satchet of falls
Come again to the falls
For a life of living falls
That makes you flow
With the loving flow
Of a profound living flow.

Bridal Veil falls-
Proudly Zimbabwean
 and profoundly Zimbabwean
Peace to all our loving visitors

harmony to the whole world
Bridal Veil falls is the whole world.

THE MOST UNSPEAKABLE

People do the most unspeakable
You find them tomorrow
Wanting to speak to you
Wanting to smile with you
Chat with you
Eating and drinking with you
Smile and smell to infinite
With you
Feel famous with you
Gallop and gossip about you
Merry making with you –
After all this unspeakable.

When money is in abundance
What happens
when money goes missing?
What happens when you smile
Without a financial smile?

What happens –
 when challenges rain
Like mvura yemakoto
 and mubvumbi rains
What happens to them?
Whilst you are eating sadza and gusha
What happens

when they see you?
BEYOND MY MEANS

Beyond my brain
I had no room
to brainstorm
Beyond my means
I had no means
To retrieve it
Without a plug spanner.
You can't remove the plug
Without a bolt cutter
There is no short cut
Without patience
Passion will never pay
Without perseverance .
You will never prosper
I had the passion
 for perseverance
I have peddled throughout
The jungles of genesis
Right up to revelation

A journey of a thousand smiles
It begins with a single smile.
Welcome aboard
My journey
of a thousand smiles.

FAREWELL FRANSISCA

Go well
Dig a well
And drink your life
For water is life

Go well
 and dig more wells
And fetch more water
And water your ideas
Dig another well
And learn to live well

AFTERMATH OF CYCLONE IDAI

Whenever it starts to rain
Everybody prays
Not for your come back
Everybody prays
For rainfall without Idai

Many souls were tormented
Many hearts were broken down
Fear lives in our hearts
Fear dwells in our souls
Cyclone Idai

May you go forever?
Farewell cyclone Idai

Go well –
never come back
Never ever come back
 To our motherland Zimbabwe
Just like corona virus
Never ever come back to Zimbabwe
Never ever land
On the Zimbabwean land.

ALLOWANCE OF LIFE

Allow love to lead
Allow hurt -
to leave you
Allow bitterness
To bid you bye-bye.
Allow love
 to love you.
Allow anger
to leave you.
Anger will never
 give you wealth.
Anger will never
make you rule.

Make yourself nice
Allow anger to escape

From your profound walk of life
Allow harmony
To harmonize you
Live with harmony –
Each and everyday.

You only live one life
You only live one love
Live one life with love
So-to get it right
Allow monopoly to leave you
Allow people to love you
Allow passion to patronise you
Allow the world to rule you
The world remains your benchmark

Set up an example
Your life is an example
Your life is an examination
Every day is an exam day
Allow Zimbabwe to examine you

ZAMBEZI WATER FOR BULAWAYO

Zambezi water
For Bulawayo
Zambezi waves

For Bulawayo –Zimbabwe
Zambezi water
That is our everyday song.

Zambezi water
We sing this song
With profound optimism
We sing this song
With great perseverance
We sing this song
With patience and passion
Passion for lasting solutions
Passion for progress everyday
Passion for people
If our people can get water
It will bring an everlasting smile.
Smile forever Bulawayo – smile!
Halala halala halaaaaaaaala!
Halala Bulawayo omuhle – halaaaala!

A journey of a thousand miles
Begins with a single step
Let's increase the steps
Let's increase whatever we can
Let's increase ideas
Let's increase solutions
Let's increase passion
Let's increase perseverance
Winners never quit
Quitters never win
Zambezi water for Bulawayo
Halala Bulawayo – halaaaala!
Halala today and forever

Halala fgorever more
Halala Bulawayo wethu –
halaaaaaaala!

Our prophecy for years
Will today come to pass.
Halala Bulawayo today –
          halaaaaaala!
U Madube ogeza ngamanzi odubo
U MaNcube ogeza ngamanzi okuncweba
U Sithole onatha amanzi angatholakaliyo
Halala Bulawayo omuhle – halaaaaaaala!
Water is coming tomorrow morning
Pure water like honey
Will be flowing like honey
From your precious tapes
In the city of Bulawayo.
Halala Bulawayo wami halaaaala!
Halala pure water halaaaala

LOVE LOOKS BETTER

Love has no passion for pizza
Those who live for pizza
Will live to eat pizza
Will want to eat pizza
And prosper for pizza
Die eating pizza .
Love has no passion
For a portion of pizza

Farewell Miss pizza
Farewell Mr pizza
Farewell Mr& Mrs pizza

Love looks better
After each and every cyclone
Go through the cyclone
Refrain from clowns
And stop being a clown
There is always a cloud
Behind every clown
A cloud beyond
every love clown

Love will look better
When you pursue patience
And passion for love
Love looks better everyday

WHAT DOES IT TAKE TO TANGO

Legends have said it all
Deeds have said it all

Words can't do more than this
Anymore
Deeds can't do more than this
Anymore
Eyes can't see

further than this
Anymore

WHEN THE CYCLONE IS GONE

There were prons and cons
Of the aftermath of cyclone Idai
Many lives were lost
Including livestock in the village
The soil and surface suffered

Gold was seen floating
 on the surface -
Of the soils of Nyabamba –Rusitu
Makorokoza rejoiced
 with simplified labour.
It was another hustle again
From all four corners of the country
Money makes noise
 when it comes to you .
Money moves
 in severe pain and silence
When it soils back to the ocean
And it leaves you
With a successful reflect of silence .

 What remains
is another cyclone of silence

Once a millionaire of money

Mills around in today `s state of criteria
Sprawling with a trillion
 of poverty and silence.

GOD IS IN CONTROL

He loves my life
He loves you too
He can do anything
at any time
He can do anything
 in the morning
And all your moaning
 goes that morning.
He can do anything
 in the afternoon
And see yourself happy
in the afternoon
He can do anything in the evening
And make your evening even.

He can do something in your sleep
A new life will start from your sleep
Sleep well
And dream well
There are so many lives
That started with a dream.
Your dreams are in your bible
Read the bible everyday
And receive life `s profound blessings.

I LOVE CHILDREN

Children are born beautiful
They don't bark
Like ageing adults
They bark beautifully
They are not sour
 or sulky
Like senior children .
They sing,
smile and soliloquies
They sing happiness
They smile to infinite
They soliloquise outside your sight

Children –
I love children
From border to border
To global village of valour
Black or white
Children are evergreen
Children are born beautiful
They harmonize our hearts
They smear us with smiles
More children less adults
More children more happiness
I love children oh
I love children
I love the lives
That bring up these children
Mothering - we salute you

Global mothers you are.

BEING A BLESSING

I was looking for a blessing
An unusual blessing
And so I prayed
For this fast and efficient blessing
There after
it came with a blessing
And to bless me
It blessed another blessing
Who is another blessing?
Does he see this as a blessing?

I am writing to you Blessing
The first blessing
Who brought us this blessing
I write to you Muzaya
So that you also get blessed
I write to you
Wherever you are
Receive the blessing
Whatever you are doing
Do it with my blessing
Whatever you try profoundly
Try it with my profound blessings.

You were blessed to bless
May you get blessed
For being a beautiful blessing

Give and you shall be given

MY PEN AND PAPER

Before anyone else hears me
I am here to hear myself
My echoes
Of life, love and laughter
I love my life
I love my life
I walk with my life
Love and living
I live to love and laugh.

A smile cemented with silence
Like a machine gun
With a built –in silencer

Before anyone else
I   live and love
I am here to live
A long life of love

Before anyone else
Decides to cry
I am here to carry
The courage
that carried my cry
The living courage
That carried my current cry

The courage
 that cured my crying

I like crying
Crying carries away
all my cry
My pen
My paper and perseverance
My passion,
 paper and persistence.

My pen and paper
Rules my precious day.
What rules your day?

I DANCED WITH THE DEVIL

I danced
and dined
 with the devil
As of yester years
Decades of years
Centuries in progress
It's time to say goodbye
It's time to say goodbye
my dear devil
Farewell my dear devil
Hapana chisingaperi
Kana maninji akapera wani

Zvinopisha zvikapora wani.

The devil is a liar
He lays eggs of lies
Fries his own eggs of lies
He fries them
 and feed you
He leads you into temptation
You see your temper flying
Know that the devil is with you
He is using you
To achieve
 his aims and objectives
He evaluates you
 and removes your value
today the devil is valueless.

There is no value or valour
In the devils evaluation .
I danced with the devil
Until he took away
 my value and valour.

I danced with the devil
Until I escaped by a whisker
God,s whisker is great
He whisks you
 from the devil,s whiskers.
Of the evil one
You will see no evil
When the devil is gone .
You hear no evil
When the devil is no more

in your life.
The devil is a liar
He lied to me
He lied using my relatives .

Life is precious with God
Life is great with God
Life is precious with the devil
You can't live without the devil
I hope the devil is listening.

You can't talk
without the evil one
Life is a journey of temptation
You have to temper
 with those temptation
Rejoice when you meet temptation
How many times
 have you been tempted?
How many times
 was Jesus Tempted?
Eat temptations
Dine with temptation
Stronger together
You grow stronger
 With the strongest temptations
You gain more strength
With increased temptation .

From power to glory
Only grace will get us there
Turn the tables everyday

Be a game changer everyday
Only Christ can make you and I
A game changer
Change from the devil
Change from the evil doings
Change from dwelling
With a dear devil
 who can devour you.
Devours your failure
Eyes on the future
Eyes on the prize of Christ
Only Christ will never – fail me.
Aluta continua with Christ.

I LOVE YOU

With a pace
Full of patience
I love you .
With a face
Full of passion
Passion for love
Passion for you
I love you.
Spores of love
Love does have spores
Soft spores of love
I love you .
Soft spores of love

I love you
I love to spoil you.
I love you
To spoil you
In your special space.
I love you
Love does have
Its frequencies
Its living modulation
I love you .
Loving you
Will leave me
With another version
Of a living love
I love you .

My life is to love you
My business is to better my love
For you and me and ourselves

I love you
Bees bring honey
I bring honey
From the bee hive
Of the bees to you .
I love you
I bring honey to you
Pure for you
I bring the honey
That I harness
From my honey
I love you
From sunrise

to sunset
I love you
I do have a bee hive
From where I live to love you
My hive is full of love

I love you
 from top to bottom
My hive is a haven of love
I love you
Even after heaven on earth
Loving you
And loving you again
With my living love
I love you
Living with you
Is like living with everything
I love you without everything
I haunt everyday
And harness honey for you
I love you honey

I live to salute you
With long lasting love
I live to love you
Throughout the days
Of my life and love
I live to love you
I live to love and live
For you
And for your love

IN SEARCH OF TRANQUILLITY

Like the one I experience
When I go through my writing spree
When I travel through
Chikwakwa
Chikukwa
Muchadziyei
Mutsangani
Bumba and Bangira
Tsholotsho and Jotsholo

Not forgetting my excursions
Through Nyamunhamba heights
Nyamutsitsi
Kwadzore
kwaDembweni neDemeni
kwaHlabiso
kwaTonhorai
Chikore and Chirinda

BUYING TIME

How do you buy time?
When should you buy time?
Where do you buy time?
Why do you buy time?
Do you smile or smell
When you buy time ?
Do you frown
or follow

When you buy time?

Time will tell
When to buy time
Or bid farewell to time.

YOU WILL FIND GOD

God will be there
Wherever you are
In whatever you will be doing
He will be doing it with you
Wherever you go
He will be there
Wherever you are
He will be there
You will find God
When God calls you
Or upon you .

If you can't see him
He will find you
If you think you are clever
He will cleanse you.
Ask Saul or Paul
If you think he can't provide
Ask Moses on his way to Canaan
If you think he is not faithful
Ask about his greatness
From the faithful ones

If you think that he is blind
Like blind Bartmeus
Ask honourable Bartmeas

GOD OF SURPRISES

God is full of surprise
Don't be fooled
 by people `s surprise
Don't be surprised
When God surprises you

Be still
And know
a miraculous God
Be still
And belong to God
Be still
And bear with God
Be still
And listen God
Be still
And God will guide you
And notice you
Today and there after

Sacrifice to stay
With God and Godliness
God will give you –
Godly surprise.
For he who endures
Right up to the end

Will be rewarded in due course
God rewards Godliness

ZIMBABWE MY ZIMBABWE

From sunrise to sunset
Zimbabwe
From first loudest cry
To my crippled cry
Zimbabwe
From my first birthday
To the day I will say goodbye
Zimbabwe

 Bury me in Zimbabwe
Bury me
in every corner of Zimbabwe
Bury me
All over Zimbabwe
Bury me
In every place in Zimbabwe
My heart belongs to Zimbabwe
My peace and patriotism
My birth right belongs to motherland
My country Zimbabwe
Bury me again in Zimbabwe
Bury me only in Zimbabwe

My optimism opts for Zimbabwe
My passion perspires in Zimbabwe

Bury me in Zimbabwe
Bury me here
In the heart of Zimbabwe
My heart belongs to Zimbabwe
My soul and soul searching
Bury me many times as you can

CLEAN UP ZIMBABWE

Cleanliness is next to God
Clean up your golden environment
Until it is cleaner
Than any other places
Clean up your town
And your rural environment
Confine litter to the bin
Confine cleanliness
to your environment
Your environment
Your pride
Our living environment
Our profound living pride

Clean up Zimbabwe
Until it is whiter than snow
Clean up Zimbabwe –Zimbabweans
Until it is cleaner
Than any other –continents
Clean up Zimbabwe
Let the sun shine

On the sunshine city
Clean up Zimbabwe
Until it is cleaner
Than any other global country

Be exemplary
Whatever you do
Wherever you go
Set up a successful example
Clean up our country

BELIEVE IN YOURSELF

Everything starts with yourself
Everything starts with you
A smile begins with you
Begin your day with a smile
And see success smiling at you
Begin your day with a package of
Love, tolerance,
 passion and forgiveness
Begin your day with patience
Patience carries your pay slip
Passion carries your destiny

NOTHING CAN STOP ME NOW

Good night and goodbye
To pessimism and pessimist

And perished along the way
My heart is full of internal way
My road of life is full of eternal joy
It is well – with me

Prosperity is the prophecy
Of a new day
A new dawn
A new era

I won't live without a destiny
I want to see death
Neither on a death before
My destiny
Destiny after another destiny
I stand here today
To declare a divine destiny

HUSTLE LIKE A MAN

Hustle like a man
And live like a man
Hustle like a lady
Live a legacy
A legacy filled with
perseverance and endurance
Hustle like a woman
Guts are gutted in women

Hustle like a woman
And lead a global light legacy

Behind every successful story
There is a woman full of coverage
Bravery and beauty

ANGER ,BITTERNESS AND EMOTION

Anger will never anger well
In everyday humanity
Angriness will bear its fruits of ugliness
When you agree to go angry
You also agree to be ugly
The two always carry mutual respect
They tour the same principles
And identical to perspective
They share the same love
And the same feelings of love
Do you love to live with anger
The choice we make today
The choices that determine our destiny
The love we live today
Is the love that leaves our legacy
Live and lead a legacy
Live and weave a legacy

Angriness agrees with ugliness
They alternate and alternate
They agree to disagree
They carry a degree of disagreement

They sit all day and disagree
They love to live in disagreement
They love to live in disharmony
They love to live without a life
I am here to live one life
A life full of laughter and love

Live life to the fullest
Do good and follow all genres of goodness

Be a good man
Man enough to live with love
Be a real woman
Full of beauty and brain
All women are born
With a profound good heart
Be a good heart –dont hurt
Be good to yourself first
Be good to everyone you meet
Today
Be good to everyone you see
Today
Be good to everyone you saw
Yesterday
Be a mother not a monster
Be a mother to your father
Be a mother to your daughter
Be a mother to your children
Remain a mother to your grand children
Be a mother to the nation
And nationalise with peace
Patriotism, optimism, purposefulness
Love will lead you to another level

Love will leave you with a level

A SERIOUS LIGHTER LOOK

I can see far
Follow me
If you want to go far
I see beyond far
Follow me
If you want to go
Beyond the horizon

Life is full of frivolity
Give it a frivolous approach
Every day of your life
Today you are a humourist
Tomorrow you are an environmentalist
Above all a patriot
Passionate about patriotism
If you are a Zimbabwean
Love Zimbabwe
Zimbabwenise
Wherever you are today

Greet life with vibrant passion
Look back with a smile everyday
Not a smeared smile
Not a borrowed smile
Prescribe to the self-sufficiency syndrome
Look forward with a profound smile
Everyday

Learn to say –thank you
Everyday
And live like a beggar everyday

Live a passionate life
Everyday
A life full of passion everyday
Passion will pay everyday
When you invest in profound passion

REFRAIN FROM BADMOUTHING

Bad mouth
Bad mouthing
It all starts from your mouth
And gradually out of your mouth
Wash your mouth
And keep a clean mouth

Bad mouth
Begins from your mouth
May you please clean your mouth
Bad words and wording
Begins from your mouth
May you please
Clean your word of mouth

Stop bad mouthing

About anything
Yourself first
Your mother and fathers
Your neighbours and community
Your country of birth
Love your country of birth
Love your neighbour
Whenever he is in labour

Always carry a bag
Full of good bread
Full of passion
Full of patriotism
Full of optimism
Optimism supersede pessimism
Perspire for optimism
Perspire for a positive passion

Speak righteous words
And walk in righteousness
Speak righteous words
About yourself
And fellow country man
Speak good everyday
About your country of birth
Whatever is pessimistic today
Is good for the optimist tomorrow

ZIMBABWE BEGINS WITH YOU

Peace begins with me here
Peace begins with you there
Peace begins with us all about

From all corners of Zimbabwe
Peace begins with everyone
Peace begins with everybody

Unity begins with you there
Unity begins with me here
Unity begins with all of us
Unite for a progressive Zimbabwe
Unite for a purpose of progress
And propel profound prosperity
Unite for a cause
And cause a cohesion of prosperity
Unite for a common cause
And cause Zimbabwe to prosper
Unite for a generation
And generate a new Zimbabwe
A new republic of Zimbabwe
Publicized with peace and prosperity
A new dispensation
Will depend on your dispensation
Let's dispense prosperity syndrome
Let's dispense peace and prosperity
Let's dispense peace and patriotism

And above all
Let us dispense love
Love for another
Love for mother land Zimbabwe
Patriotism begins with you me
I will love Zimbabwe
I will love mother Zimbabwe
I will love mother Africa
I am proud to be an African

I am proud of being an African
God bless Africa
God bless the continent of Africa

Patriotism begins with you
Love Zimbabwe
Zimbabwenise Zimbabwe
Zimbabwe is you
Zimbabwe is me
Zimbabwe is all of us

Patriotism is peace
Peace upon Zimbabwe
Patriotism upon Zimbabwe
Patriotism is the politics of love
Love Zimbabwe
From day one
Love Zimbabwe
From day one
To number one

Love Zimbabwe today
Love Zimbabwe and make it great
Love Zimbabwe
And make Zimbabwe
Number one destination
Of your destiny
Number one destination
Of peace and tranquillity
Number one destination
Of an egalitarianism society
Number one destination
Of international cultural heritage

Number one destination
Of every living tourist
Number one destinations
Of a harmonized environment
Number one destination
Of prosperity dispensation

allow patriotism
To patronise you
Allow love to lead you
Allow peace
To penetrate you
Allow unity
To unite us
Allow leaders
To lead us
If you are a follower
Follow Zimbabwe
If you are an optimist
Believe in Zimbabwe
Bholato-bhalato
Asante Sana –Zimbabwe
Aluta continua –Zimbabwe

FOCUS ON YOUR PURPOSE

Have focus –
Do you have focus?
Purpose

Do you have a purpose?
A purpose in life
A purpose for your life
You were created with a purpose
You were created for a purpose
Live for that purpose
Live with that purpose in mind

Every minute – remind yourself
Everyday – go back to your senses
Don't become weaker –
Each and every week.
Every month –
Maintain momentum.
Every year you must yield results
And throughout your entire life
Live and lead a legacy
Live and live a legacy

Every dog can bark
Don't react to every dog
 that barks.
Every dog has potential to bark
Never react to any potential dog.
Life is not all about barking
Its also about silencing
The dogs that are not barking properly,

Focus on your purpose
In your real life
Focus on today
And tomorrow's life
Focus on life

And its greatness to you.

Focus on Christ
And his exemplary life
A journey of humanity
It begins with Christ in your life.

COME CLOSER TO DAD

I want to feel your presence
I want to feel your warmth
Please come closer to me
Come closer with me

I want to feel your peace
Nothing supersedes your peace
Come closer to me - everyday
I want to feel your optimism
I want to refill you with optimism
Come closer for more optimism
I want to fill you with patriotism
Your community begins
With your patronage
Your country begins
With your patriotism
Come closer to me
So that I can baptise you
With profound patriotism.

Come closer to Dad
I want to feel you with love
Want to refill you with love and laughter
When you pay attention
You are filled with
 patience and attention
Come closer for
 more patience and attention

come closer tyo Dad
I want to reduce
your volume of anger
there is no market for anger
there is no market for pride
there is no market for your emotions
I want to get rid of your emotions.

Come closer – to me
And become a fully fledged human being
Free from persistent pride and arrogance
Free from persistent pessimism
Free from – persistent inhuman attitude.

WHEN GOD IS SILENT

God is never – silent,
When God is silent,
He is busy – talking to you

Listen to your God
When he is busy talking to you.

He talks through the Bible
Read the Bible
Listen to the Bible
Obey the Bible
God speaks through the Bible
He talks to you –
Through events and people
Keep in touch with people

When God is Silent –
He is doing something in silence.
Do something for him in silence.
Do something – to bless you
Do something
That gives you blessings.
Do something different
That graces you with grace
Do something
that gives you grace
If you ignore grace –
You shall be disgraced.
When you receive faith
You shall remain faithful.

When God is silent –
He is saying something.
Something so   precious
Something awesome
Something unbelievable

God's silence is your prosperity
 so keep your eyes on the prize
your prayer will never -
paralyse you.

I LOVE HIM FOREVER

I love him I love him
I love him
He is my greatest God
I love him forever.
God gives
And he has given me.
God answers
And he has answered me.
God always smile – at me
God's smile
Is the best smile.
God's purpose
Is the best purpose.
God's time
Is the best time
This is God's time.

God's smile
is the best for me,
and he has never
run out of smile.

I love you
I love you
I love you
My ever lovely God
My ever living God

My God lives
And loves me
My God does everything
        For me
He is a God of everything
I love you
I love you
I love you my God
I love you for – everything
I love you
For this precious life
Life is the best gift
You can ever have.
I love you
I love you
For this precious life I have.

BYE BYE CONT MHLANGA

Bye bye !

Bye bye Cont.

Bye bye – bye!

I am the first one –

To miss you

Whoever comes after me

Is second .

Bye bye Cont –bye!

The village of Lupane

They will miss you

Amakhosi Township Square –

Umkhulu lomsebezo!

We are here to celebrate you

Today we celebrate your walk

You talked as you walked

Today we celebrate love

Love for theatre

Thank you for your humor

That harmonized us

The city of Kings –

The city of Bulawayo

KoBulawayo

City of Kings and Queens

This city will miss you

The ordinary man on the street

The vendor of tomatoes and onions

Makokoba township will miss you

Makokoba – khula uze ukokobe.

Makokoba will miss you

Cont Mhlanga

Siyabonga Mhlanga

Drama will never be the same

You had your own taste of uniqueness

The voice will never be the same

You had your own voice

You had a life to live

You lived it second to none.

You were full of passion

Nothing can beat passion

Nothing can beat patience

Nothing can beat ;patriotism

We continue to patronize – patriotism

Zimbabwe my Zimbabwe

I love you – Zimbabwe

Zimbabwe for Zimbabweans

Zimbabwe for Africa

Zimbabwe for the global village
Britain for the British

China for them the Chineese

America for the Americans

Europe for the Europeans

Africa for the Africans

I love Zimbabwe –

Day and night

I love Zimbabwe

Before I go to bed

I love Zimbabwe

Wherever I am

And wherever I go

Sikju nesikati

Zimbabwe yangu Zimbabwe

Zimbabwe my Zimbabwe

Bye –

bye – my fellow Zimbabwean

Bye bye – Cont weZimbabwe

Bye bye Cont weLupane

Bye bye the global Cont Mhlanga

You wrote as you lived

We wrote – together

You did all that you did –

With passion – passion

Be passionate –

Whatever you do todasy.

Follow your passion –

And your happiness –

will follow you .

follow your passion

and your success will

follow you.

Pursue your passion –

And your passion will live

To satisfy you.

Thank you – for yoiur passion

You inspired many

Many more are yet to be inspired

Thank you for the noise –

That went beyond our nose.

Bye bye - Cont kaMhlanga

Until we meet again

Halala halala halaaaaaaala!

Halala halala beyond our echoes

Until we meet again –

Bye bye – bye!

Halala Halala – good bye

Theatre at the graveside –

      In Lupane

Its time to say goodbye Lupane

Goodbye Lupane

Good bye ZIMBABWE

Good bye

The last celebration

For a profound celebrity.

Aluta – continua

Umkhulu lomsebenzo!

I AM A GAME CHANGER

I am - a game changer

Where there is a hole,

I am putting a borehole.

Where there is wood,

Lets work with the wood.

Where there is land

Let's land on the soil.

Son of the soil,

Let's make use of the soil.

Daughter of dawn

Let's get down before dawn.

I am a game changer

Lets thrive to change the game

I will bring in a pain killer.

There are millions and millions

Of pain killers.

Happiness on its own

Is a pain killer.

A profound smile

On it's own

It's a painkiller.

Real love

On its own

It's an amazing -

Pain killer.

A SON LIKE YOU

One daughter

One son.

A son like you

Groomed with manners

Manners begin from home.

One son like you

Groomed to know God

Groomed to love God

Groomed to care-

Care begins at home

Respect itself begins from home.

ONCE UPON A TIME

You are born - once

You live – once

You die – once

You love – once

You marry only – once

You smile more than once

So keep smiling more than once.

You laugh more than once

Laughter is the best medicine

Laughter is the only prescription

Be – happy

Wherever you are

Be happy all the time,

Always put on a smile

Never lose your smile

Your smile is everything

  everyday

be happy

everyday of your life

be passionate – about life

be passionate about love

be passionate about your parents

parents come first

they brought to you here

to this mother earth

may you please come down

    to earth.

be passionate about first family

be passionate about people

LOVE ME LOVE ME

Love me

Love me

love

Love me

The way you love

 Yourself.

Love me

The way you love

Your mother

Love me

Love me

Like your living mother

Love me love me

Like your lovely mother

Love me

Like your living sister

Love me 'beyond your sisters

And your brothers

Love me

Love me

Love me

 beyond your children

Beyond heaven and earth.

Love me

Till death do us part

Love me

Love me

With all your love.

Love me

Love me

Beyond measure.

Love me

And I will love you

I will love you

Forever.

TOO BLESSED –

Too blessed –

To be stressed.

Too busy –

To be disturbed.

Too blessed

To worry

And remain sorrowful.

Too blessed

To think about the past

Past is past

Waiting for the future.

Past is past

Looking in the future

My past is my past

My past remains my story

That is my history.

Too blessed

To retain and attain

    Hatred.

too blessed

to go about

without a laugh

and a profound smile.

Too blessed

When I give

And forget.

Too blessed

When I give

And forgive.

I am too blessed

Wherever I am

I am blessed

Wherever I go.

I get blessed

When I walk

And talk

Get blessed

When you walk

And talk.